Pleasant Words
and A Coin

By Aleksandar Hemon

The Question of Bruno

Nowhere Man

Aleksandar Hemon

Exchange of Pleasant Words and A Coin

PICADOR SHOTS

![Macmillan logo]

First published 2006 by Picador
an imprint of Pan Macmillan Ltd
Pan Macmillan, 20 New Wharf Road, London N1 9RR
Basingstoke and Oxford
Associated companies throughout the world
www.panmacmillan.com

ISBN-13: 978-0-330-44581-8
ISBN-10: 0-330-44581-2

1 3 5 7 9 8 6 4 2

A CIP catalogue record for this book is available from
the British Library.

Typeset by Intype Libra Ltd
Printed and bound in Great Britain by
Mackays of Chatham plc, Chatham, Kent

Exchange of
Pleasant Words

I

WHAT YEAR WAS IT? We have chosen to believe it was 1811. Therefore: in the autumn of 1811, Alexandre Hemon got up from his slothful bed in Quimper, Brittany; sold, unbeknownst to his widowed mother, their only horse – a perennially exhausted nag – for thirty silver coins; and joined, after some adventurous drifting, Napoleon's army on its way to Russia, heading for yet another glorious victory. He was, we believe, twenty-one at the time. We imagine him marching through Prussia, still stunned by the greatness of the world; crossing the Nieman river in June of 1812, the river washing down a gossamer coat of dust

3

and cooling off his sore, blistering feet. Then we can see him charging at the ferocious Russians at Smolensk. At Borodino, he leads the infantry attack armed with a sabre; he single-handedly captures a battery of begging-for-mercy Russians. ('No, Lev, that was not a victory!' my father might exclaim when narrating this particular stretch of the family history.) We watch with him the flames of Moscow scalding the sky's belly. But there's no joy any longer in his extinguished heart: the victories don't seem so wholesome any more, and his sore feet have changed state – now they're frozen solid. Then comes the humiliating, murderous retreat. The officers are nowhere in sight, the soldier next to you just soundlessly drops in the snow like an icicle, then never gets up, and the Russians keep mauling the mutilated body of the great army. He stumbles and falls through the snow-laden steppe and when he raises his head he's in the midst of a thick forest.

We know very well that the route of the Napoleonic army's retreat went through what is today Belorussia, and there's no plausible explanation for Alexandre ending up in western Ukraine, near Lvov. Certain factions in the family suggested that higher forces had had a hand in the miraculous (mis)placement of Alexandre. My father – who deems himself the foremost authority on the family history and one of its main narrators – dismisses the implausibility with a derisive frown, providing as evidence a map of Ukraine, dating from 1932, on which Smolensk (for example) is just inches away from Lvov.

Be that as it may, Alexandre went astray from the straight road of defeat and found himself, unconscious, in the midst of a pitch-dark forest. He drifted to the edge of the eternal black hole, when someone pulled him out of it, tugging his benumbed leg. There's hardly any doubt that that was the great-great-grandmother Marija. Alexandre opened his eyes and saw the angelic smile of a seventeen-year-old girl trying to take off his decrepit, yet still precious, boots. Let me confess that a blasphemous thought has occurred to me: the angelic smile might have been seriously deficient in a considerable number of teeth, due to the then-common winter scurvy. She, naturally, decided to take him home, unloading the fire-wood and mounting him on the tired nag (somehow, that was the epoch of tired nags). Her parents, surprised and scared, could not resist her determination, so she made him a bed near the hearth and then nursed him out of his glacial numbness, patiently rubbing his limbs to get the blood started (Uncle Teodor sometimes likes to add a touch of gangrene at this point). She fed him honey and lard, and spoke to him melli-fluously. Yes, she rekindled his heart and they did get married. Yes, they're considered to be the Adam and Eve of the Hemon universe.

My mother, who proudly descends from a sturdy stock of Bosnian peasantry, considered all this to be the typical 'Hemon propaganda'. And she may well have been right, I'm afraid to say. For we have no well-established facts from which the unquestionable existence of Alexandre Hemon would necessarily follow. There is, however, some circumstantial evidence:

a) At the time of the Winter Olympics in Sarajevo, my sister held in her hand a credit card in the name of a certain Lucien Hemon. Lucien was the rifle manager for the French biathlon team. He told my sister, not hesitating to flirt with her, that Hemon was a rather common family name in Brittany and suggested, after she had managed to tell him the highlights of the family history, that a Napoleonic soldier could have well carried it over to Ukraine. That was the germ from which Alexandre sprung, and the previously dominant theory that 'Hemon' was a Ukrainian variation on 'demon' was indefinitely suspended.

b) In 1990, a busload of excited Bosnian Ukrainians went to Ukraine in order to perform a set of old songs and dances, long forgotten in the oppressed ex-homeland. While they were staying in a waterless hotel in Lvov, the Hemons decided to venture into the village (Ostaloveschy) that my great-grandfather's family had left to move to Bosnia. I should point out that a widespread belief in the family was that we had no kin in Ukraine. As they snooped around the depressed village, mainly populated by bored-to-senility elderly folks, they aroused plenty of suspicion among the villagers, who must have believed that the KGB was on to them again. In antique Ukrainian, just for the hell of it, they questioned toothless men leaning on their canes and fences about Hemons in the village, until one of them pointed peevishly at the house across the dirt road. The man in the house told them that, yes, he was a Hemon, but had no knowledge of any kin in Bosnia. He told them outright that he was no fool and that he knew they worked for the police. They tried to dissuade him from throwing them out, pointing out that police agents and spies do not move around in such large and compact groups – there were fourteen of them, all vaguely resembling one another and scaring the wits out of their poor distant cousin. Next day, the man (his name was, not surprisingly, Ivan) visited them in their dismal hotel, considerately bringing a bottle of water as a present. They told him, trying to outshout each other, about the exodus to Bosnia, about the family bee-keeping, about the legendary Alexandre Hemon. Yes, he told them, he might have heard about a Frenchman being related to the family a long time ago.

Thus it was definitely established by the family that our tree was rooted in glorious Brittany, which clearly distinguished us from other Ukrainians – a people of priests and peasants – let alone Bosnian Ukrainians. Once Alexandre Hemon was officially admitted to the family, the

interest for things Gallic surged, and no one much
cared for the nuanced differences between the
Bretons and the French. My father would
unblinkingly and determinedly sit through an
entire French movie – French movies used to bore
him out of his mind – and then would claim some
sort of genetic understanding of the intricate
relations between characters in, say, *A Bout de
Souffle*. He went so far as to claim that my cousin
Vlado was the spitting image of Jean-Paul
Belmondo, which consequently made Vlado (a
handsome blond young man) begin referring to
himself as 'Belmondo'. 'Belmondo is hungry,' he
would announce to his mother upon returning
from work in a leather-goods factory.

Further developments in the Hemon family-
name history were propelled – I'm proud to say –
by my literary exploits. In the course of attaining
my useless comparative literature degree at the
University of Sarajevo, I read the *Iliad* and found
a lightning reference to 'Hemon the Mighty'.
Then I read *Antigone*, where I discovered that

Antigone's suicidal fiancé was named Hemon – Hemon pronounced as Haemon, just like our family name. In the agon with Creon, Hemon at first looks like a suck-up:

> My father, I am yours. You keep me straight
> with your good judgement, which I shall ever
>   follow.
> Nor shall a marriage count for more with me
> than your kind leading.

But then they get into a real argument, and Hemon tells Creon off: 'No city is a property of a single man,' and 'You'd rule a desert beautifully alone,' and 'If you weren't a father, I should call you mad.'

My father dutifully copied the one page from the *Iliad* that, towards the bottom, had 'Hemon the Mighty' and the handful of pages in *Antigone* where the unfortunate Hemon agonizes with the cocky Creon. He highlighted every sighting of the Hemon name with a blindingly yellow marker.

He kept showing the copies to his co-workers, poor creatures with generic Slavic surnames, which – at best! – might have signified a minor character in a socialist-realist novel, someone, say, whose life is saved by the fearless main character or who simply and insignificantly dies. My father didn't bother to read *Antigone*, never mind tens of thousands of lines of the *Iliad*, and I failed to mention to him that 'Hemon the Mighty' is absolutely irrelevant in the great epic, or that Antigone's illustrious fiancé committed not-so-illustrious suicide by hanging.

The following semester, I found a Hemon in the *Aeneid*, who makes a fleeting appearance as a chief of a savage tribe. Sure enough, my father added the promptly highlighted photocopy to his little Hemon-archive. Finally, in *Gargantua and Pantagruel* I stumbled upon 'Hemon and his four sons' involved in an outrageous Rabelaisian orgy. The Rabelais reference, however, provided the missing link with the French chapter of the family history, which now could be swiftly reconstructed all the way back to 2000 BC.

There is, unfortunately, a shadow stretching over this respectable history, a trace of murky, Biblical past that no one dared to follow but that the designated, though inept, historian feels obliged to mention: My cousin Aleksandra still remembers the timor and terror she felt when, in church, she heard the priest utter – clearly and loudly – our name. The priest, she says, described a man who stood in the murderous crowd under the cross on which Our Saviour was expiring in incomprehensible pain, his eyes (the man's, of course) bulging with evil, bloodthirsty saliva running down his inhuman chin, laughing away Our Saviour's suffering. 'What kind of man is he?' thundered the priest. 'What kind of man could laugh at the Lamb's slaughter? *Hemon* was his name, and we know that his seed was winnowed and scattered all over this doomed earth, eternally miserable, alone and deprived of God's love.' Stricken with horror (she was nine), she retched and ran out, while her father, my uncle Roman, who was not paying attention, kept saying 'Amen!'

Later investigations found no Hemons in the Bible, although it is entirely unclear who the researcher was and how exactly the research was conducted. The official explanation, accepted by the entire family, was that the priest was performing an act of vicious revenge, probably because my aunt Amalija called him 'a pig in the vestment' while the wrong ears were listening, or because my father married a communist.

In any case, few thought that we carried the mortifying burden of the ancient sin on our shoulders, or that we would have a family reunion in hell. 'We have always been honest, hard-working people,' my father announced to the priest who replaced the hostile one (who had moved to Canada), pointing his finger towards the ceiling, beyond which, presumably, there was the supreme judge and avenger. The priest amicably nodded and accepted a bottle of home-made slivovitz and a jar of first-class honey, with which the potentially eternal dispute between the Hemons and God (regarding his Son) was settled, it seemed then, satisfactorily for both parties.

I have had doubts, however, along with some of my younger cousins and a very close relative. I have had doubts and fears that indeed we could have committed the terrible sin of sniggering at someone else's suffering. Perhaps that's why we emigrated, again, in the 1990s, from Bosnia to the United States. Perhaps this is the punishment: we have to live these half-lives of people who cannot forget what they used to be and who are afraid of being addressed in a foreign language, no longer able to utter anything truly meaningful. I have seen my parents, mute, in an elevator, in Schaumburg, Illinois, staring at their uncomfortable toes, stowed in foreign shoes, as a breezy English-speaking neighbour entered the elevator and attempted to commence a conversation about the unkind Midwestern weather. My father kept pressing the buttons '11' and '18' (where the

verbose American was heading), as if they would
terminate the fucking multilingual world and take
us all back to the time before the Tower of Babel
was unwisely built and history began to unwind
in the wrong, inhuman direction. My mother
occasionally grinned painfully at the confounded
neighbour, as the elevator rose arduously, through
the molasses of silence, to the eleventh floor.

2

Inspired by the success of the Sarajevo Olympiad
and the newly established ancient family history,
the family council, righteously headed by my
father, decided to have an epic get-together, which
was to be held only once, and was to become
recorded as the Hemoniad. The minutes from
that family-council meeting (taken by me) can
scarcely convey the excitement and joyous awareness of the event's future importance. Allow me
to step out of my historian's shoes (one size too

small) and become a witness for an instant: I can attest that there was a moment of comprehensive silence – a fly was heard buzzing stubbornly against the window pane; fire was cracking in the stove; someone's bowels disrespectfully grumbled – a moment when everyone looked into the future marked by the Hemoniad, the event that would make our Homeric cousins envious. Even Grandfather, in one of his precious lucid moments, seemed to recognize everyone and did not ask, 'Where am I?' The magic was dispelled when the milk-pot boiled over, and a swarm of aunts flew towards the stove to repair the damage.

Thus it was decided that the Hemoniad was to be held in June 1991, at Grandparents' estate, which was falling apart because of my grandfather's dotage, but was, nevertheless, 'the place where our roots still hold the land together, fighting cadaverous worms'. It was also decided that the Hemons should reach out to the Hemuns, the family branch that grew out of the tree trunk of Uncle Ilyko, my grandfather's brother.

This is their history: Uncle Ilyko went from Bosnia to Ukraine to fight for Ukrainian independence in 1917. After the humiliating defeat, in 1921, he walked to the newly-formed border between Romania and Yugoslavia, where they arrested him and put him on the train back to Kiev. He jumped off the train, somewhere in Bukovina, and then roamed, as the first snow of the year, ominously abundant, was smothering the earth. He almost froze to death, but was found and saved by a young war widow, who nursed him out of glacial darkness all winter, asking for nothing from him, but to warm her cold feet and dilute her loneliness. In the spring, he got up from the shaky bed, took from her trembling hands a bundle with knit socks, a brick of cheese, and her daguerreotype. He kissed her tearful cheeks, including a hirsute wart, and walked, only at night, back to the Romanian–Yugoslav border. Sometime in the spring of 1922, he swam across the Danube, whose murky, cold waters dissolved the daguerreotype.

Well, we never liked him. He was a violent, impetuous man. The day Ilyko returned home – where everyone thought he had long been dead – he got into a fight with Grandfather, because my grandfather had married the girl Ilyko had had a crush on. Infuriated, he went to Indjija, Serbia, married a native, and let a drunken clerk change his name to Hemun, which became the original sin of the Hemun branch. Indeed, the Hemuns avoided contact with the descendants of my grandparents, barely spoke Ukrainian, sang no Ukrainian songs, danced no Ukrainian dances, and thought of themselves as Serbs. The Hemuns, then, were to be saved from 'the weed of otherness', and come back to 'the forest of flesh and bone growing out of the ancient Hemon roots'. When they told Grandfather that the Hemuns were to come back to their historic home, he – God bless him – asked, 'And who are they?'

In the weeks after the family-council meeting, the invitation was forged in the Olympic minds of Uncle Teodor and my father. Uncle Teodor made suggestions, and my father rejected them as he typed. Let me submit an image: Uncle Teodor running different formulations by my father: '. . . the branch that was unjustly severed . . . the branch that fell off and broke the tree's heart . . . the branch that shrivelled, detached from its roots . . .' My father's index fingers leaping up and down the typing keyboard, like virgins dancing for gods – Father occasionally using a virgin to pick his nose, and saying, 'No . . . no . . . no . . . no . . .' Like all the great documents of history, the Hemoniad invitation went through many drafts and finally attained the form of exceptional grace and power. It clearly stated the purpose ('. . . to reattach the most formidable branch to its just place . . .'); the place ('. . . the Hemon family estate, where thousands of years of history are told by bees and birds and chickens . . .'); the logistics ('. . . we shall feast on spit-roast piglets and mixed salad, and if you need cakes and pastry, you are advised to make them yourselves . . .'); the structure ('. . . spare time will be spent in the house, in the courtyard, in the backyard, in the field, in the orchard, in the apiary, in the garden, in the cowshed, by the creek, in the forest, in conversation and exchange of pleasant words . . .'). The invitation was gladly received by many, and responses from all corners of the family began pouring in. The participation of many Hemuns was heralded by a phone call from the oldest Hemun, Andrija, and a tide of elation advanced through the family. Oh, those days when planning a piglet slaughter over the phone had mythological proportions; when old stories were excavated from the basements of memory, and then polished and embellished; when sleepless, warm nights were wasted in trying to make sleeping arrangements, until Uncle Teodor suggested the hay under the cowshed roof, where 'the youth' could sleep; when my mother kept rolling her eyes, suspicious of any mass-meeting of people of the same ethnicity; when aunts independently met to organize the cake and pastry production, lest we have a surfeit of *balabushki*.

I'm afraid this sentence was inescapable: the day of the Hemoniad arrived. A huge tent had been put up, above a long table. The stage for 'the orchestra' had been built under the walnut tree in the centre of the courtyard. Uncle Teodor, they say, was up at dawn, sitting on the porch and rehearsing the stories for the last time. I woke up (allow me to interpolate a personal memory) to the incessant warbling of birds nesting under the roof. When I descended the stairs, I saw a pair of dancing headless chickens, trying to run away from something (but couldn't because it was everywhere), their wings arrhythmically flapping, blood spurting out of their necks in decreasing streams. We had breakfast, sitting around the big table, passing panfuls of fried chicken livers and hearts, and platefuls of sliced tomatoes and pickles. 'This', said Uncle Teodor, 'is the greatest day of my life.'

The Hemuns arrived all at once, with a fleet of shining new cars, like a colonizing army. They were uniformly overweight and spoke with a northern-Serbian drawl, which implied a life of affluent leisure. Nonetheless, everyone hugged each other, cheeks were smacked with kisses, hands were shaken ardently, and backs were slapped to the point of bruising. Uncle Teodor hollered, 'Welcome, Hemuns!', and then proceeded from Hemun to Hemun, offering them his stump. He would turn his ear to each of them, asking, 'And who are you?' and then memorize their voices.

The day went on in an agreeable atmosphere of general merriment and pleasant conversing. We have pictures, recorded on tape, of the crowd in the tent, milling in a perpetual attempt to get closer to each other, like atoms forced to form a molecule, while everyone perspired, merging into one big body, with moist armpits and indestructible vocal cords. The band played all day, on and off, sovereignly led by my cousin Ivan, who kept winking, over his heavily-breathing accordion, at every woman under forty not directly related to him. When the band played old Ukrainian songs, the Hemuns sat grinning, confounded and embarrassed, for they could not understand a word. But everyone danced in whatever way they could, waltzing clumsily, their hands adhering to their partner's bobbing sides and sweaty palms; or, their stage fright temporarily cured by an infusion of a helpful beverage (beer was my choice), they would dance *kolomiyka*, spinning at different speeds, from neck-breaking to mere circular trotting.

Around one o'clock, as the sun got stuck right above the walnut tree top to serve as stage light, my six aunts ascended the stage, having been introduced by Uncle Teodor, who recited their hypocoristic names like a poem: 'Halyka, Malyka, Natalyka, Marenyka, Julyka, Filyka.' They sang a song about a young Ukrainian soldier who was being sent off to die in yet another battle for the freedom of Ukraine, and he was doing what most of the soldiers in most of the Ukrainian songs did all the time – he was saying goodbye to his inconsolable mother and his faithful bride-to-be. They sang (my aunts) with their arms akimbo, serenely swaying and rubbing each other's elbows. They looked like six variations of the same woman. Grandfather suddenly pricked up his ears, as if recognizing the song, but then he was retaken by the demons of slumber and succumbed with a grunt. Meanwhile, the soldier died (as we all had expected) and his faithful bride-to-be was about to be ravished by the same force that was to enslave Ukraine. 'This song', explained Uncle Teodor, after my aunts bowed, blushed and scuttled off the stage, 'is about the value of freedom and independence.'

Then the lunch was served, and everyone sat around the long table, with Grandfather floating on the Lethe at its head. The table was creaking under heaps of pork and chicken limbs. There were big-ear soup bowls, which were reverently passed around the table, as steam was enthusiastically gushing up, like smoke from a snoozy volcano. There were plates of green onions, stacked like timber, and tomato slices sunk in their own slobber. After the lunch, everyone became drowsy, descending from the mountains of meat to the lowlands of sleep. Snippets of conversation died off within seconds, for no one's blood was capable of reaching the brain. Grandfather was fast asleep and snoring, leaning on his sage stick. He burped in his sleep and moved his tongue over his upper lip, touching the bottom of the moustache, and then in the opposite direction along the lower lip, for a whiff of pleasant taste had escaped the inferno of slow digestion and reached his palate. Finally, everything yielded to the stupor, and excited flies could land, after a long journey, on the continent abundant with meat and salad. They would comfortably sit on a slice of bread, greasing themselves to dazzling summer-fly glitter. Abruptly they would ascend, as if to check whether they could still fly. They would go down again, buzzing messages of festive pleasure to each other. Watching them, it occurred to me that they were our flies – Hemon flies – and therefore better than other flies, oblivious to their historical role.

On the videotape of the Hemoniad, the only document of the glorious festivity that reached the United States, this transcendental torpor is contained within three or four intense minutes of silence, the hum of the breeze in the microphone notwithstanding. It is important to note, however, that the flies disappeared in the process of converting the tape from PAL-SECAM to NTSC.

Then Uncle Teodor was snatched out of his wheezing tranquillity and led to the stage, where he was ushered into a chair. The level of consciousness abruptly rose around the table. Uncle Teodor said, 'I will tell you stories now, because it is important to know one's own history. If you know the stories, just sit quiet and listen – we have people who don't know them.' The Hemuns – people who didn't know the stories – fidgeted and glanced at each other, for they suspected that the stories would present them as treacherous and weak people. But Uncle Teodor had different intentions. He began with the Hemons of the *Iliad*, their doughty feats and their contribution to the burning of Troy. Then he talked about the Hemon who almost married Antigone, the most beautiful woman of the ancient world. He barely touched on the Hemon who was Aeneas' sidekick and who founded the Roman Empire with him. He talked about Hemons defending European civilization from a deluge of barbarian Slavic marauders. Then he skipped a number of centuries and nearly brought tears to everyone's eyes talking about the murderous retreat and Alexandre's travails and the horrors of the Russian winter. He told us of Alexandre's hallucinations: armies of headless men, marching in circles, and he trying to escape a gigantic axe that strived to decapitate him, until he fell down – 'He didn't feel the snap, but he felt blood spurting and the cold slowly gnawing his limbs.' And then he was saved by our Ur-Mother Marija. As Uncle Teodor was narrating their budding love and Alexandre's recovery, Grandfather burst to the

28

surface of the day, looked around in genuine astonishment and asked me, since I was sitting next to him:

'Who are these people?'

I said, 'They're your tribe, Grandpa.'

'I've never seen them in my life.'

'Yes, you have, Grandpa.'

'And who are you?'

'I'm one of your grandchildren.'

'I've never seen you in my life.'

'Well, now you can see me.'

'Where are we?'

'We're home, Grandpa.'

That seemed to satisfy him, so he dropped his head to his chest, and was back in the boat crossing the Lethe. In the meantime, Uncle Teodor got to Alexandre and Marija's progeny. The Hemons of the mid-nineteenth century were all invariably bright and dextrous and hard-working, but they seemed to have perennially suffered from Polish and Russian injustice, plus tuberculosis and scurvy. Moreover, women kept miscarrying, while men kept falling from trees and being gored by disobedient cattle. 'And yet we survived!' exclaimed Uncle Teodor. He went on to tell a story I had never heard before, a story about the ancestor who had gone to America to become a rich man, and when he became a rich man he returned to his village. He built a beautiful house and did nothing but court rural virgins, receive guests, and drink with them. One of his guests, probably the devil incarnate, dared him to spend a night in the local graveyard, which was known to be haunted by the village Jews massacred in a pogrom. He bet his whole estate that he would spend the night and he did, but he met the rosy-fingered dawn with his hair completely white and his hands unstoppably shaking. He never told anyone what he had heard or seen, but the next day he gave all he had to the rabbi of the few remaining Jews so he could build a home for the wandering spirits. He was deemed insane after that by his relatives, who had just got used to being members of a wealthy family, and who claimed that it was Jewish magic that had cast a spell on their dear cousin. One day he disappeared, and no one ever saw him again. Uncle Teodor claimed that he had gone back to America, and that we probably have some American cousins. As we imagined our half-mad hoary cousin sailing towards the Statue of Liberty, coffee was served. We sipped strong tarrish liquid from a demitasse, without really noticing that Uncle Teodor had omitted the second half of the nineteenth century (probably because some of our forefathers were prone to pogrom fever) and began telling the well-known narrative about the exodus to Bosnia.

Imagine the crushing poverty, the year-long drought and cattle plague, the bone-cracking cold of the 1914 winter, the widespread banditry of hungry, destitute ex-peasants – we all writhed in our seats, fretting over the unforeseeable future with our ancestors. Great-grandparents Teodor and Marija, the story went, packed all they had: a few bundles of poorly patched clothing; a beehive, sealed to make the trip; some clay pots and a coal iron; a roll of money they had saved up, which spent the trip in my great-grandmother's bosom absorbing sweat and entertaining lice. Grandfather, presently dozing off next to me, and Ilyko fought, throughout the journey. He told us how they had been given a piece of uncultivated land – 'this very land' – which was now 'the best piece of land in Bosnia', although, to tell the truth, it produced nothing but retarded corn and shrivelled apples. Great-grandfather went to Sarajevo to get the papers for the land on the day the Archduke Franz Ferdinand was killed. He bought an accordion there, 'this very accordion', which was not true, for Uncle Teodor himself had crushed the accordion some years ago. Oh, the years of struggling and working from sunup to sundown. And then Ilyko went to fight the Bolsheviks – 'We all know what happened then, and that is why we are all here now.'

It was the Hemuns who got impatient first, and

their impatience quickly became contagious. As Uncle Teodor, entirely carried away, continued talking about Uncle Julius and his twenty-five years in Stalin's camps, both the Hemuns and the Hemons kept rising, hastening towards the outhouse, pouring slivovitz down their throats, chitchatting, anything but listen to the blind narrator. By the time Uncle Julius got to the Arkhangelsk camp, where he was to be sentenced to death, no one – except me – was listening. My father stood up and said, 'Enough, Teodor. You'll continue later.' But he never did, for the band started playing again and everybody was imbibing elating beverages. Again, shoulders were slapped, crushing hugs and smacking kisses generously exchanged, while dancing, even if in slow motion, seemed to be approaching trance. Some of it can be seen on the videotape, but not without effort, because I had one drink too many, and the camera was held by my tremulous hands. Thus the image is shaking and tilting, which, incidentally, could well render everyone's giddiness. As

the camera was taken away from me to be shut
off, so was my clear-mindedness, and everything
became dizzy and dim. Allow me to submit
several discontinuous memories – memories of
images and sensations that flashed before the
helpless mind's eye, as the mind capsized and
sank to the sandy bottom of complete oblivion:
the noxious, sour manure stench coming from the
pigsty; the howling of the only piglet left alive;
the fluttering of fleeting chickens; pungent smoke,
coming from moribund pig-roast fires; relentless
crunching of the gravel on which many feet
danced; my aunts and other aunty women tread-
ing the *kolomiyka* on the gravel, their ankles
universally swollen, and their skin-hued stockings
descending down their varicose calves; the scent
of a pine plank and the prickly coarseness of its
surface, as I laid my cheek on it and everything
spun, as if I were in a washing machine; my
cousin Ivan's sandalled left foot tap-tap-tapping
on the stage, headed by its stocky big toe; the vast
fields of cakes and pastry arrayed on the bed (on

which my grandmother had expired), sorted meticulously in chocolate and non-chocolate phalanxes; the intense, chewy taste of green onions and pork that washed off my palate, immediately followed by a billow of gastric acid; greasy itchiness around my mouth, adumbrating numerous, putrid pimples; the hysterical, aroused, chained dog leaping at me, nearly choking himself and coating my hands and face with his drool; the seething warmth of the concrete steps, in the proximity of the dog, where I attempted to regain my sea-sick consciousness; the needly hay under the revolving roof of the cowshed; my hand holding a long, crooked stick (a Napoleonic sword), beating a nettle throng (Russian soldiers), and my forearms burning and rubicund; truckloads of helmeted soldiers, passing by the house, shooting in the air, and showing us the three-fingered sign, shouting and throwing bottles at chickens; trucks dragging erected cannons, and dark jeeps following them; an unfamiliar cat, caught as it was stealthily jumping on the table strewn with gnawed bones and splinters of meat, staring at me, the pupils stretched to the edges in utter feline disbelief, as if I were not supposed to be there, as if my vomitous existence had not been approved by the potent being whose approval the cat clearly had.

Then I was sitting down on the grass, leaning against the walnut tree, then closing my eyes and carefully searching for the position in which my head would stop gyrating. I put the tips of my index fingers against my temples, and thus fixed my head, not daring to blink, let alone to move. I heard the din of voices, the garrulous babel, the uproar of guttural excitement, which all eventually ebbed. Then I could hear (although I'm not sure I did) my father's voice, 'wishing to conclude this epic festival of Hemonhood, with words that could not possibly match the greatness of the occasion'. He talked about our ancient roots and 'thousands of years of Hemonian diligence', which helped us survive the biggest catastrophes in human memory. 'Do you think it is an accident that our ancestor Alexandre was one of the few to survive the unfathomable defeat of Napoleon's army? Do you think it is just luck that he progressed through several heart-chilling blizzards to meet the woman of his life, the Eve of the Hemon universe?' No one dared to answer these questions, so he went on and on, and talked about the courage it took to move to Bosnia, 'the wild frontier of the Austro-Hungarian Empire'. He dwelt for some time, as I was successfully resisting retching, on 'the progress that we brought to these parts' with 'civilized bee-keeping, iron plough and carpentry skills'. We built 'our empire out of nothing', and it was 'no accident that our grandfather met with the Archduke before he was assassinated – our stock is heroic and royal'. He told us (although I was barely there) that we should 'read the Greeks, the founders of the Western civilization' if we didn't believe – 'We're all over the history of literature.' So he proliferated thoughts about the family history, mentioning names that I could not attach to faces any more – they all merged into my grandfather who was presently and perpetually passing in and out of nothingness. I do not know where our greatness ended – if indeed it ever ended – for I passed out. Then I heard energetic applause, a choir of hands clapping and clapping, and someone was slapping my face. As I opened my eyes, everything rushed away from me, except the face of my mother, who said, 'It seems that the history wore you out. Do you want to vomit?'

My mother led me away, while I mismanaged my steps, from the tumultuous tribal space, holding my right arm above the elbow, and I felt her swollen, arthritic knuckles squeezing my muscle. 'The trouble with the Hemons', she said, 'is that they always get much too excited about things they imagine to be real.' I was wobbling, looking at the prows of my feet, imagining the straight line that I had to follow so as not to appear drunk. But then I simply closed my eyes and let my mother steer me around chairs and chickens and buckets and tree stumps and flower beds.

'I made a terrible fool of myself,' I said. 'You're almost a man now,' she said. 'And that is a man's privilege.'

She made me sit under a shrivelled apple tree. Small, wizened apples – not unlike my brain at that moment – hung like earrings from crooked, exhausted branches. My mother sat down by my side and put her arm around me. I wanted to put my head in her lap, but she said, 'No, you'll just get dizzier.' We could hear the Hemons-Hemuns hollering against the music, which from a distance sounded discordant. We could still hear the trucks, and I vaguely realized that they had been passing by all day. 'I wish these trucks would stop,' I said. 'They probably won't for a while,' my mother said. Her hands smelled of coffee and vanilla sugar. She told me about the time her father gave their only horse away.

'It was in '43 or '44, a young man came running out of the corn. Mother and Father knew him, he was lank and had blue eyes, a Muslim from a nearby village. He said that the Chetniks had killed his whole family, that he escaped, leaping through a window, and now they were after him. He had a bruise on his cheek, as if someone had kissed him with plum-lips. He asked my father for the horse so he could get away and join the partisans. Father glanced at my mother, she said nothing, but he knew and he went to get the horse, cursing all along, "Fuck this world and the bloody sun and this country when everyone needs my horse." The young man, his name was Zaim, kissed both of my father's cheeks and promised he would return the horse once the evil had blown over. So he rode off, waving at us. But then the Chetniks came, riding their horses, like cowboys, down the road. "Where is he?" they yelled. "Where's the circumcised dog?" And my father said, "What's the trouble, brothers?" They all had beards and rifles and knives. They shouted, "Did you see the Turkish bastard?" Father said, "I don't know who you're talking about." "You're lying!" they yelled. "You're a traitor!" Then they beat him with rifle butts, they threw him on the ground and kicked him with their boots. "What's wrong with you, motherfucker, you're one of us? Where's the Turk? Who's he to you?" I thought they would slit our throats, no problem. My brother was in the partisans, but we spread the word that he was in Srem, working.'

'You've never told me this,' I said.

She continued: 'They kept beating him until he was bleeding and unconscious. My mother wept and begged them to spare him. Then one of them, beardless, came to me and said, "There's a little Serbian girl who is going to tell us where the Turk is." Oh, I couldn't say a word, and then I saw my mother's eyes, frightened, and her hands squeezing the strength out of each other. I told them I hadn't seen anyone and that I would tell them if I had. So they left, and the beardless one told us that he would personally judge us if he found out we were lying. That was our only horse, you know, all we had.'

I resisted falling asleep, trying to keep my eyes open, but then I succumbed, leaning on my

mother's shoulder, even in my dreams aware of
the possibility of disgorging myself. I slept for
hours, thinking in my troublesome sleep that I
was leaning on my mother, but then I woke up,
with my cheek on a molehill, sprawled on the
ground covered with rotting apples. I went back
to the yard and all the Hemuns were gone, as if I
had dreamt them; and everyone else, scattered
around, was cleaning up, storing away the food
or taking the tent and the stage apart. I need not
have been there to know what happened at the
end. It can all be seen on the tape, which we
occasionally watch when I visit my parents in
Schaumburg, Illinois. We rewind and fast-
forward, to get to the moment we most want to
cherish. We freeze the frame to remember a name,
we fill in the gaps, caused by unwarranted cuts
and blanks thanks to a ten-dollar conversion in a
Pakistani store on Devon. Frequently, there's a little tide of fractious dots rising from the bottom of
a trembling picture, always trying to reach the
centre. Finally, the last image is of my mother, just

about to say something – something irreverent about 'the Hemon propaganda', perhaps. That is all too clear from her clever eyes and the lingering, undeveloped grin. She never says it, forever on the verge of saying something. She can never remember what she was going to say, and the screen suddenly turns blindingly blue, and we turn it off and rewind the tape to the beginning.

A Coin

SUPPOSE THERE IS A Point A and a Point B and that, if you want to get from Point A to Point B, you have to pass through an open space clearly visible to a skilful sniper. You have to run from Point A to Point B and the faster you run, the more likely you are to reach Point B alive. The space between Point A and Point B is littered with things that sprinting citizens have dropped along the way. A black leather wallet, probably empty. A purse, agape like a mouth. A white plastic water-vessel, with a bullet hole in its centre. A green-red-brown shawl ornamented with snow-flakes, dirty. A wet loaf of bread, with excited ants crawling all over, as if building a pyramid. A video cassette, dismembered, several of its pieces still connected with a dark writhing tape. On days when snipers are particularly rabid, there are scattered bodies as well. Some of them may still be alive and twitching towards the distant cover, leaving a bloody trail behind, like snails. People seldom try to help them, for everybody knows that the snipers are just waiting for that. Sometimes a sniper mercifully finishes off the crawling person. Sometimes the snipers play with the body, shooting off his or her knees, feet or elbows. They seem to have made a bet how far he or she is going to get before bleeding away.

Sarajevo is a catless city. It is so because people couldn't feed them, or couldn't take them along when they were fleeing, or their owners were killed. Hence the dogs that couldn't be fed or taken along hunt them down and devour them. One can often see, among the rubble on the streets, underneath burnt cars, or stuck in sewers, cat carcasses, or cat heads with a death grin, eye-teeth like miniature daggers. Sometimes one can

see two, or more dogs fighting over a cat, tearing
apart a screaming loaf of fur and flesh.

*Aida's letters are scarce and sudden, escaping the
siege via UN convoys, foreign reporters or
refugee transports. I imagine them in a sack, in
the back of a UN truck, driven by a Pakistani
or Ukrainian soldier oblivious to everything but
the muddy road before him and the gaze of the
bearded thugs by the road, their index fingers
conspicuously close to the trigger; or a letter in a
reporter's bag carelessly thrown over a tattooed
shoulder, sharing the bottom of the bag with
a walkman, notebooks, condoms, bread and pot
crumbs, and a wallet crammed with family pictures. I imagine letters in a post office in Zagreb
or Split, Amsterdam or London, in the midst of a
pile of letters sent to people I know nothing about
by the people who care about them. Sometimes it
takes dismal months for her letters to reach me,
and when I open my mailbox – a long tunnel
dead-ending with a dark square – and find Aida's*

letter, I shiver with dread. What terrifies me is that, as I rip the exhausted envelope, she may be dead. She may have vanished, may have already become a ghost, a nothing – a fictitious character, so to speak – and I'm reading her letter as if she were alive, her voice ringing in my brain, her visions projected before my eyes, her hand shaping curved letters. I fear to communicate with a creature of my memory, with a dead person. I dread the fact that life is always slower than death and I have been chosen, despite my weakness, against my will, to witness the discrepancy.

In September, Aunt Fatima passed away. She had had asthma for a long time, but in September she just asphyxiated in our apartment. They were pouring shells for weeks on end, and even when they didn't there was an eager sniper. He killed our neighbour who hadn't even left the building. He just peeked out of the door, cautiously ajar, and the bullet hit him in the forehead and he dropped down dead. Anyway, Aunt Fatima ran

out of her asthma medicine, and she couldn't go
out. The windows had been shattered long ago.
She was always cold, breathing in cold air satur-
ated with floating dust. She simply suffocated,
producing that inhaling, sucking sound, and
nothing was being inhaled. We couldn't bury her,
or even take her out, because they kept shelling
and sniping as if there was no tomorrow.

Kevin is an American, from Chicago. He's a
cameraman. He's been around, he says. He's been
in Afghanistan and Lebanon and the Persian Gulf
and Africa with his camera. He's tall, his arms are
little hills of muscles. His eyes are greenish, like
dried turf. He has two parallel silver earrings in
his left ear. His hair is short. He's balding and has
a peninsula of greyish hair crawling down his
forehead. He's lean. When you look closely, you
can see purple ruptured blood vessels where his
nose meets his face. It's from cocaine. He did it a
lot in Lebanon. It was cheap and he broke down.
He couldn't stand it any longer. An Arab child

shot at him with what he took to be a toy gun. There is a scar-furrow on his thigh. He was new, he broke down, he did cocaine. Now he's fine, he says. I like him because he tells stories. All of those people do, all those reporters and cameramen and all those who have been around. But they're all clichés, as if they watched too many movies about foreign correspondents and war reporters. Kevin's stories are different. All those others always tell stories about other journalists. A British drunk, a German ex-Nazi, a French sissy, an American whore, are stock characters. They never tell stories about the local people, because the natives are news, they're what's to be reported. Kevin told me stories from Afghanistan, about lying in a high mountain ambush with bearded rebels. And about terrified Russian convoys crawling up a dire mountain road, knowing they're being watched. About a Russian soldier being cut in pieces alive, producing unreal shrieks, until a merciful *mullah* shot him in the head. He filmed it, even though he knew they would take the tape away from him. Even if they didn't, it would've never been broadcast.

She sent me a black and white picture: she is standing on a pile of debris in the midst of the library ruins. I could see holes that used to be windows, and pillars like scorched matches. The camera looks at her from underneath: she is tall and erect, as if on the top of a mountain; she is in a bulletproof vest, wearing it detachedly, as though it were a bathing suit.

I've got this job as a liaison for the pool of foreign TV companies. Besides helping them to get by in hell, to approach and bribe government officials and find good parties, I edit footage that crews shoot in and around the city. Then I send it via satellite to London, Amsterdam, Luxembourg or wherever. I get two to three hours of footage every day. It's mainly blood and gore and severed limbs. I cut it into fifteen to twenty minutes, which are then transmitted to the invisible people who edit it into one to two minutes of a news story, if there is one. At the beginning, I was trying to choose the most telling images, with as much blood and bowels, stumps and child corpses as possible. I was trying to induce some compassion or understanding or pain or whatever, although the one to two minutes that I would later recognize as having been cut by me would contain only mildly horrific images. I've changed my view. I stopped sifting horror after I saw footage of a dead woman being carried by four men. She was prone on their arms, as if on a hearse. As they were carrying her, her head was bent backwards, hanging down. Her skull was cut open by a piece of shrapnel. There was a skull-sod with hair, hanging on a patch of skin. They put her in the back of a truck, with other heaped corpses. Her head was still open. I could see the brainless bloody cavity. Then one of the men closed the cavity, putting the sod back into its place, as if putting on a lid. He did it with a certain reluctant respect, as though he was covering her naked body, as though there was something indecent in seeing the inside of somebody's head. I cut all that out and put it on a separate tape. From then on I was cutting out everything that was as horrid. I put it all on one tape, which I hoarded underneath my pillow made of clothes. There once was that corny idiotic movie *Cinema Paradiso*, where the projectionist kept all the kisses from films censored by a priest. Hence I christened the tape 'Cinema Inferno'. I haven't watched it entirely yet. Some day I will, paying particular attention to the cuts, to see how the montage of death attractions works.

I had a dream: a woman alone on the glowing screen, and a moat in front of it, and beyond the moat is a room, windowless, full of people. She is performing me, she is acting me out. I'm in the audience, sitting in a row at the end of my gaze, on the verge of darkness. She's not doing it right. This is not how I felt, this is not my pain. I want to get up and scream, and tell her that she's much too involved in myself. She's even attaining my shape, my face, my voice. I want to help her step out of me. But I can't do anything. She's a light mirage. I can't get up, because I don't know what exactly is wrong. And then I realize – it's the language. I'm confined within the wrong language.

Pure-bred dogs can be seen running in packs or, seldom, alone. You can see German shepherds, Irish setters, Belgian collies, Border collies, Rottweilers, poodles, chow chows, Dobermanns, cocker spaniels, malamutes, Siberian huskies, everything. After years of siege, there are, naturally, many mongrels. Some of the breeding combinations would amaze, or terrify, a canine expert. In the winter, when every living creature is in the middle of starvation, dogs are more inclined to move in packs, often attacking with common strategy, like wolves. There have been occasions when an improbable mixture of dog races attacked a child or a feeble elderly person. A German shepherd would be going for the throat, a poodle would be tearing the flesh off the calves.

It is after I write her a letter with trite reminiscing that I begin wanting to tell her all about me – I have imaginary conversations with her, making real grimaces, gesturing with real hands. I think of all the things I could've told her or should've told her: how awkward and cumbersome I feel in English, sinking in syntax, my sentences flapping helplessly, like a drowning child's arms; about Bach's St Matthew Passion; about desiring the arrival of spiders – the vicious cockroach-killers – in my living space; about the lack of relationship – or contact, rather – with women; about the friendless immigrant life; about the Headline News *I keep watching, waiting for a glimpse of Sarajevo; about my Western window, looking at corny sunsets and the distant O'Hare Airport, night aeroplanes landing like tired firebugs; about an involuntary memory I had of my father smashing with a shovel a nest of infant mice; about the fact that almost everything I wanted to tell her is not in the letter; about the sense of loss and the damp stamp-glue taste lingering on my tongue for hours after I drop the letter in the mailbox. I used to believe that words could convey and contain everything, but not any more, not any more.*

I grew fond of Kevin because he never openly showed me his affection. He would just tell me stories. Even in a room full of people, I knew the stories were for me. I liked him because he was so detached. He said it was the 'cameraman syndrome', always being a gaze away from the world. We're not in love, love is out of the question. Nobody's in love in this godforsaken city. We just keep learning about each other. We just share stories, becoming a story along the way. And the story may end at any moment. When we make love, in the darkness – no electricity – it's harsh and cruel, as if we were fighting, because we have to wrestle joy and flashes of love from our irked bodies. We never talk about his future departure. He has callused feet, from marching through the Afghanistan mountains.

After some grotesque obsequies, we put Aunt Fatima in my room. It soon became *her* room. None of us would go in there. When something was needed from her room – a scarf, a blanket, a photo – someone would say, 'It's in Fatima's room,' which meant it was irretrievable. We kept hoping that we would be able to bury her, but a week passed and she was still there – my malodorous aunt.

On Tuesday I had a sensation (a hallucination?) of cockroaches scurrying up my shins – I may be losing my mind, because of the solitude and nothingness that constitute my life. I had the sensation at a rock show, while boys and girls shook their heads like rattles. I thought that the cockroaches were my home-grown cockroaches, that I brought them with me from my apartment, unknowingly. The next day I asked Art, my janitor, to help me

*and he gave me those roach-motels in which
roaches get lured by sweet syrup and then get
stuck in glue. Let's put it this way: Art provides
room for abhorrent insects, Art terminates cockroaches.*

I hate Kevin. He brought footage of yet another
massacre: people crawling in their own blood,
faceless skulls, limbs strewn, stuff like that. There
was this woman, her arms were severed. You
could see two frayed, blood-spurting stumps. She
was raising the bloody mess of her ex-arms
towards Kevin's camera. Kevin had a close-up of
her face, still in shock, not feeling any pain, not
being armless yet. The close-up lasted for a good
five minutes, like fucking Tarkovsky. I asked
Kevin why didn't he drop the goddamned camera
and help the woman. He said there was nothing
he could do. He's a cameraman, he said, and that
is what he does and how he helps people. I told
him he shouldn't have shot that close-up. He said
he didn't do it. It was his camera who did it, he

A Coin

just held it. I cut it out anyway. I put it on the
Cinema Inferno tape. Nobody saw the footage
but me. Kevin is so detached and so protected.

I sleep in a former TV studio, next to the editing
room. It is windowless, of course, safe from
shelling, unless they use concrete-piercing shells.
Which they seldom do, for whatever reason. I
suppose that even such a shell wouldn't kill us
immediately. It would just open a hole for more
shells. I prefer to die immediately. The studio has
a little stage where mindless folk singers used to
perform their play-back love pain. This is where
we sleep, as if on a raft – on a stage soaked with
false tears and real sweat. There are still several
cameras in the studio, with their lenses turned
to the floor, looking between their wheels, as if
ashamed. The studio is immense and very dark.
We light it with two strategically positioned
candles. There is some electricity in the building,
to be sure, produced by a coughing gasoline-run
generator, but we need electricity to produce and

render false images. We move around the studio as if blind, having a memory of the studio as the map in our heads. We never move cameras, lest we run into them and get hurt. But somehow they always get in our way, as if they're moving silently behind our backs, like ghosts, recording us.

I've been sending letters for her through obscure Red Cross channels – it takes months for a Red Cross convoy to reach Sarajevo and even more for my letters to reach her. When they do, they're already obsolete, they're rendering someone other than myself, someone saner – a stranger not only to her but indeed to myself. When I'm writing those letters I have to accept my helplessness, I have to admit that someone else is writing them, using my body, my Pelikan fountain pen, my cramped right hand. Whatever I write, I feel it to be untrue, because it'll be untrue in a day or two, if not in a moment or two. Whatever I say I am lying or will be lying. On the pages of the letter, the whiteness of the page stained with ink, a dismal present descends into a desolate past. That is why I tend to write her things that she already knows, tell her stories told wars ago. It is cowardly, I confess, but I'm just trying to create an illusion that our lives, however distant, may still be simultaneous.

The odour escaped Fatima's room whatever we tried to do. We stuffed the cracks between the door and the frame with rugs. We soaked the rugs and the door with vinegar and our useless perfumes (Obsession, *Magie Noir*). But the stench was always there – the sweet, dense, meaty scent of decay. In the midst of a rare and brief nocturnal lull in shelling, we decided to throw her out of the window, after my mother woke up screaming, having dreamt maggots coming out of her sister's eye sockets.

Kevin and I, we get drunk over his stories, with bourbon that he keeps fetching from somewhere. He tells me then what he considers to be intimate things: about his long-time girlfriend, who was working as a real estate agent, having a dream of becoming a Congresswoman. She was from a place called White Pigeon, Michigan, fifty miles south of Kalamazoo. While he was in the Gulf, she left him a message on the answering machine about leaving him because he was a 'selfish dreamy idiot'. He tells me how he sees everything through a viewfinder. He has confidence in the camera objective. He feels natural with his camera, because 'with the camera I see nothing alone'. There's always another pair of eyes, he says.

A friend of mine asked me to help her identify some damaged buildings in Sarajevo; she sent me photographs hoping that I could recognize the buildings, but they were unidentifiable as far as I was concerned. They all looked the same: they all had shattered windows – black holes, as if their eyes had been gouged; there were rings of debris around them, as if ruins were being carved out of

whole buildings; there were no people in the pic-
tures. What was in the pictures was not buildings
– let alone buildings I could've come in or out of
– but absences: what was in the pictures was what
was not in the pictures – the pictures recorded the
very end of the process of disappearing, the noth-
ingness itself.

People stand in line at Point A, waiting for their
turn to run across. When it's your turn, you
cannot wait, you have to go, because the longer
you wait, the readier the sniper is. Plus you don't
want to share the unspeakable fear of the waiting
throng. The first time I ran from Point A to Point
B, the fear was unspeakable indeed. Pain in your
stomach, as if a big steel ball is grinding your
bowels. Blood throbbing in your neck veins. Wet
heat inside your eyeballs. Numbness of your
limbs, increasing as you're running. Sweat
trickling down your cheeks, like a miniature
avalanche of dread. You see no life unwinding
before your eyes. All you see is one or two metres

before you and all the little things that you can trip over. You hear every tiny sound. Your feet brushing away dirt and rubble. Distant detonations. Cries of scared and wounded people. Whistling ricocheting bullets. The death rattle from the person behind you.

This is me in what's left of the library. If you could magnify this picture sufficiently you could see motes levitating around me – cold ashes of books. This picture was made on the day I got the bulletproof vest. It was one of the happiest days of my life, this life. A bulletproof vest significantly increases your (well, my) chances of survival. The sniper has to shoot you in the head to kill you. Which is why I cut my hair so short, to make my head smaller. Sometimes I feel like a fucking Joan of Arc, except I have no army and no voices to guide me.

Mother and Father wrapped her up in a bed sheet, and then another one, and then another one, their faces distorted by the urge to vomit. I couldn't watch when they actually pushed her over the window sill, but I heard the thud. I thought, as if remembering a line from a movie, Her life ended with a thud.

Since April I have received no letters from Aida. From that time on I had to make up her letters, I had to write her letters for her, I had to imagine her, because that was the only way to break the siege and stay connected with her. I'm sure she's alive, I'm sure that one of these days I'll have a bundle of her consecutive letters stowed in my mailbox, I'm sure she's writing them this very moment.

This war, my friend, is men's business. The other day I heard a 'joke': 'What is a woman?' – 'The stuff around the pussy!' The men in the camouflage uniforms thought it was so hilarious that they kicked the floor with their rifle butts. I sensed that the joke was for me. We're expected to remain silent, spread our legs, breed more warriors and die with motherly dignity. I think what I fear the most is rape. When a sniper bullet hits you, your body and yourself die simultaneously. Provided, naturally, that you're killed instantly. Which you usually are, because they're so fucking good. But I don't want my body to be mutilated, mauled, violated, and I don't want to witness that. When I'm gone I'd like to take my body with me. Have you heard about the rape camps?

When I got this job, I moved to the TV building, going home only occasionally, to check if my parents were alive and well. I'd usually go on Sunday afternoons, after the morning transmission of Friday leftovers. But then I stopped doing that because I realized that my local sniper was waiting for me. Before I ran, everything was silent, and several people ran across the parking lot without being shot at. When I started crossing it, bullets buzzed around me like rabid bees. He watched me. He knew I was coming. He waited for me and then toyed with me. Now I go to see them at different times, using different routes, trying to appear differently each time in order to be unrecognizable to the sharpshooter, who could be one of my ex-boyfriends for all I know.

While my head was still on the pillow, my nightmare not completely erased by the sudden awakening, I opened my eyes and saw a cockroach running from the stove, over the grey kitchen floor tiles, getting on the carpet, running a bit slower, as if on sand, going beneath the chair, coming diagonally towards my futon, going around my slippers, trying to reach the safe space underneath my futon. I watched it, it was running fast, never stopping, going straight without hesitation. What was it running from? What was running that little engine? Desire to live? Fear of death? The instinctive – perhaps even molecular – awareness of the gaze of the supreme sharpshooter? What a horrible world, I thought, when every living creature lives and dies in fear. I

reached for my left slipper, but the cockroach was
already underneath the futon.

Snipers often kill dogs, just for fun. Sometimes
they have competitions in dog-shooting, but only
when there aren't any targetable people on the
streets. Shooting a dog in the head gets you the
most points, I suppose. One can often see a dog
corpse with a shattered head, like a crushed
tomato. When snipers shoot dogs, anti-sniping
patrols refrain from confronting them, because of
the permanent danger of a rabies epidemic. When
an unskilled, new or careless sharpshooter only
wounds a dog and the dog frantically ricochets
around, bleeding, howling, biting anything that
can ease the pain and fear, a member of the anti-
sniping patrol might even shoot the dog, aiming,
as always, at the head.

The other day I took Kevin on a tour of my
favourite places in Sarajevo. He took his camera.
What I like about Kevin is that you don't have to

explain everything to him. He just sees what you want him to see. What's more, he doesn't say that he understands. You just know. We both knew, for instance, that the places on our tour were between being a memory and being reduced to nothing but a pile of rubble. The camera was recording the process of disappearing. There is a truce in place these days, which always scares me a bit. Partly because silence is often more terrifying than the familiar relentless noise of shelling. Partly because I'm afraid that Kevin might get bored and leave. Which is why, I suppose, I took him on the tour. He followed me with his camera like a shadow. I showed him our school. I stood in the wrecked window of our classroom and he shot me waving to his objective. I stood on the corner from which Princip shot those historic shots. My little feet were fitting, as always, into the concrete shapes of his feet. I took him to the few bars we used to frequent. Some of them were closed – the owner dead or something – and some of them were full of black-marketeers and men in uniform, their rifles conspicuous on the bar-stand before them. I took him to the park, now treeless – desperate firewood demand – where I used to take boys and make them touch my breasts, while they were too pusillanimous to go further. I told all that to the camera, and he circled around me, his knees bent, as if genuflecting. And then I told him, as I am telling the invisible you now, that I was pregnant.

Then we watched over it, the white pile that used to be my aunt, from the window that was hidden from snipers. We watched the bundle of decomposed flesh, as if we were at a wake, but a wake for something other than Aunt Fatima, and transcendentally important nonetheless. We would take turns, we would have shifts. Father even asked me, taking his shift, if everything was all right. I said, 'No, nothing will ever be all right.' I'm terrified with the calmness, even if ostensible, with which I'm telling you this. I feel I might burst out into madness.

A Coin

In the corners of my room, there are elaborate cobwebs, but I haven't seen any spiders. It seems that the cobwebs have a purely symbolic function – they're there to remind me that I am trapped and that, at any given moment, a tooth or a sting will inject poison into my body and then suck out my blood. The space I inhabit becomes me – the room speaks about me, as if the walls were pages of a book and I were a hero, a character, somebody.

So I had the morning shift. And right after it dawned, I saw a pack of dogs coming towards us. There was a Rottweiler, a poodle and several mongrels. They tore the sheets and I turned my head away, but I could not leave my ludicrous observation post. The only thought I remember having was about skiing. I had a vision of myself coming down the slope, going very fast, and air slapping my cheeks, and the sound of the skis brushing snow away, like a speeded-up recording of waves. When I looked out again, I couldn't look at the place where the corpse was. I looked around it, as if making a compromise. I saw the Rottweiler, trotting away, with a hand in his jaw. I wish I'd had a camera so I wouldn't have to remember. I'm sorry I had to tell you this.

My hair is all grey now. How is Chicago? Write, even if your letters can't reach me.

With a lightning move of my hand superbly handling the knife, I split the cockroach in two: the front half continued running for an inch or two and then started frenetically revolving around the head; the back half just stood in place, as if surprised, oozing pallid slime.

I woke up bleeding, in a bed soaked with blood, by the Heathrow Airport, in an expensive bland hotel, having waited for Kevin for more than a week. Kevin who didn't even bother to call me. I tried to reach him in Amsterdam, Paris, Atlanta, New York, Cyprus, even Johannesburg, leaving messages and curses. But then I just wiped myself off and went back to Sarajevo, leaving a heap of bloody towels and bed sheets, an empty refreshment bar, a broken glass in the bathroom and an unpaid bill, to Kevin's name, with his Cyprus address. So here I am now, un-pregnant, as sanguine as ever, but never as sad.

I bought a Polaroid camera to explore my absence, to find out how space and things appear when I'm not exerting my presence on them. I made snapshots – glossy still moments with edges darker than the centre, as if everything is fading away – I made snapshots of my apartment and the things in it: here's my ceiling fan not revolving; here's my empty chair; here's my futon, looking like somebody's just got up; here's my vacuous bathroom; here's a dried cockroach; here's a glass, with still water not being drunk; here are my vacant shoes; here's my TV not being watched; here's a flash in the mirror; here's nothing.

When you get to Point B, the adrenalin rush is so strong that you feel *too* alive. You see everything clearly, but you can't comprehend anything. Your senses are so overloaded that you forget everything before you even register it. I've run from Point A to Point B hundreds of times and the feeling is always the same but I've never had it before. I suppose it is this high pressure of excitement that makes people bleed away so quickly. I saw deluges of blood coming out of svelte bodies. A woman holding on to her purse while her whole body is shaking with the death rattle. I saw blood-streams spouting out of surprised children, and they look at you as if they'd done something wrong – broke a vial of expensive perfume or something. But once you get to Point B everything is quickly gone, as if it never happened. You pick yourself up and walk back into your besieged life, happy to be. You move a wet curl from your forehead, inhale deeply, and put your hand in the pocket, where you may or may not find a worthless coin; a coin.